SHINE-A-LIGHT
PRESS

For permissions, please email Shine-A-Light Press at info@ShineALightCorp.com.
Shine-A-Light Press and related logo are registered trademarks of Shine-A-Light, Corp.

Copyright ©2021, Baron D. Hall
Book edit, layout and design by Chris and Andrea Elston

Educators and librarians, for a variety of teaching tools to use with this book,
visit us at www.shinealightpress.com

First paperback edition published by Shine-A-Light Press and printed in March 2021

Summary:
When a fledgling eagle wakes on the 4th of July, he wants to get straight to the celebrations! But he learns there is a lot more to this awesome holiday than parades and fireworks.

Library of Congress Control Number: 2021932389

ISBN 978-1-953158-98-7
50899

9 781953 158987

Printed in the U.S.A.
U.S.A. $8.99

THE F4ITH OF JULY

Written by Baron D. Hall

Illustrated by Madalyn Spires

Find the hidden Liberty Bells!

The Liberty Bell is an iconic symbol known around the entire world. The religious inscription (from the King James version of the Bible) near the top of the bell is one of many examples illustrating how God's Word influenced the founding of the United States of America. The inscription reads:

PROCLAIM LIBERTY THROUGHOUT ALL THE LAND UNTO ALL THE INHABITANTS THEREOF

Can you find a Liberty Bell hidden on each spread?

Fun Facts

🔔 The Liberty Bell was originally called the State House Bell.

🔔 The bell was shipped to the colonies from London, and it cracked on its first test ring.

🔔 John Pass and John Stow melted that bell and casted a new one from the same metal.

🔔 No one knows for sure when or how the remade bell cracked.

🔔 The Liberty Bell was sent across the country in the 1800s for display at fairs and other events.

🔔 Although it is often claimed, there is no evidence that the Liberty Bell rang or cracked on July 4th, 1776.

🔔 In addition to its symbolism of general liberty, the Liberty Bell also represents the abolition of slavery, women's rights, and other historical freedoms.

Wake up, little bird! It's the 4th of July.
Stretch out your stiff wings. It's time to fly high!

Why must we leave now, so early today?
The fireworks don't start 'til late anyway.

You're right about that, and fireworks are fun.
But why do you think we celebrate, son?

It's our country's birthday, and that's why we cheer.
It's one of my favorite times of the year.

That answer's not bad but only half true.
I think there's some things that we should review.
Let's fly over there, on top of that rock.
It happens to be a great place to talk.

In 1620, a long time ago
A ship docked near here. What's its name? Do you know?

The Mayflower, right? I've heard that before.
But please keep going, I want to know more.

The Pilgrims had many reasons to sail over here.
one was to practice their faith without fear.
They came here from England, to be far from the king.
He bossed them around. That was his thing.

They stayed here and grew. They made colonies.
Thirteen were formed, but it wasn't a breeze.
Tensions kept rising, from excessive taxation—

But I want to know about the start of <u>this</u> nation.

Let's fast forward, then.
I'll give you your fix.
It happened in 1776.

The people who lived here,
they'd had enough.
They thought that the king
was being too rough.

He bullied and taxed.
He was so unfair.
The people knelt down
and asked with a prayer:

"God, what should we do? We tried some protests.
We threw out some tea that was loaded in chests."

They needed a document. It had to be bold.

DECLARATION

To make a clear statement for all to behold.

Thomas Jefferson was one who could write.
They called upon him, and he said, "All right!"

It was given a name that had to make sense:
The Declaration of Independence.

This escalated ongoing war with the Brits.
And soon after that, King George called it quits.
America was its own country—yippee!
Courageous and brave, its people were free.

This all makes sense now, and yet I feel sad
That we've had to fight for freedoms we've had.

I understand, son, but don't be upset.
With God by our side, we'd beat any threat.

Let's watch the fireworks but first the parade,
celebrating how our country was made!

Timeline of events in *The F4ith of July*

⭐ 1620—Although the land now known as the United States of America had already been discovered by Europeans, around 100 "Pilgrims" set sail on the Mayflower from England to reach the Americas.

⭐ The Mayflower sailed for over two months before reaching the shores of Cape Cod.

⭐ Although the passengers of the Mayflower landed at Plymouth Harbor, many of the Pilgrims stayed aboard the ship while explorers were sent to the mainland.

⭐ More than half of the ship's passengers died during their first winter in the this "New World."

⭐ Although the book mentions that colonies were then formed, Virginia had already been established as the first colony years before the Pilgrims arrived on the Mayflower. The others were formed after the Pilgrims arrived.

⭐ The original colonies were founded in this order:

Virginia (first)	New York	New Hampshire	Massachusetts	
Maryland	Connecticut	Rhode Island	Delaware	
North Carolina	South Carolina	New Jersey	Pennsylvania	Georgia (thirteenth)

⭐ The story fast-forwards to 1776, but many events led to the Declaration of Independence:
- 🚩 The Stamp Act (1765)
  - ★ British Parliament imposed a tax on goods purchased by the colonies, which upset the colonists greatly.
- 🚩 The Boston Massacre (1770)
  - ★ A disagreement between a British soldier and an apprentice wigmaker erupted into a crowd of hundreds of colonists harassing several British soldiers. The soldiers suddenly fired into the crowd, resulting in several deaths.
- 🚩 The Boston Tea Party (1773)
  - ★ The British government forced the colonists to purchase tea from England. To protest this, a group of colonists disguised themselves as Native Americans and destroyed thousands of pounds of tea by throwing it into Boston Harbor.
- 🚩 The Coercive Acts (1774)
  - ★ In response to the defiant act of destroying the tea, the British Parliament passed several restrictive laws. One such act required the colonists to pay for the housing and feeding of British troops who occupied their towns.

◼ Lexington, Falmouth, and Norfolk (1775-1776)

★ A plot by British soldiers to capture leaders Sam Adams and John Hancock and destroy their gunpowder was foiled when spies got wind of the plan and warned the colonists. There were several deaths in a gunfight at Lexington. The British Navy then attacked the towns of Falmouth and Norfolk, which united the colonies against the British. These events are considered the start of the American Revolutionary War.

★ Thomas Jefferson was selected to write the first draft, and he gets most of the historical credit for writing the Declaration of Independence, which would officially announce the formation of the United States of America.

★ United States independence was formally declared on July 2, 1776, but Congress did not approve the final text of the Declaration of Independence until July 4, 1776.

★ The Declaration of Independence was not signed until August 2, 1776.

★ John Hancock, being the President of the Congress, was the first to sign the Declaration of Independence. His signature is famously known for being bold and visible amongst the signatures.

★ The flag depicted in the third-to-last spread represents the United States-French Alliance Flag, which was flown around 1781-1782 to honor the end of the American Revolutionary War and to recognize aid received from France.

★ While the vast majority of the fighting ended around 1781, the Revolutionary War officially ended in 1783 when Great Britain recognized the United States as its own country by signing the Treaty of Paris.

★ The monument in the second-to-last spread represents the Bunker Hill Monument, which commemorates the Battle of Bunker Hill. It rests near Boston and resembles the Washington Monument in Washington D. C.

Were you able to find all the Liberty Bells? If not, here are a few hints:

🔔 Not all of them are colored
🔔 Some of them may be behind things
🔔 A few of them are tiny

Dr. Baron D. Hall is a practicing orthodontist from Southern Indiana, but when he's not straightening teeth, he spends his free time playing video games, making TikTok and YouTube videos, and writing books. His debut picture book, Emma Gets Braces!, was released in 2017 (*Mascot Books*). Baron is the proud uncle of illustrator Madalyn Spires. You can learn more about Baron and his upcoming works by checking out his website and social media accounts:
www.barondhall.com
YouTube.com/BaronDHall
TikTok: @thecrazyorthodontist
Twitter: @BaronDHall
Facebook.com/BaronDHall

Madalyn Spires is currently a high school student and Varsity cheerleader. When she's not studying or practicing her cheers, Madalyn enjoys painting and drawing, which has always been a part of her life. When Baron Hall, her uncle, asked her to illustrate The F4ith of July, she was more than thrilled. Along with her art, Madalyn enjoys traveling, baking, and running a comedy YouTube channel.

CPSIA information can be obtained
at www.ICGtesting.com
Printed in the USA
BVHW021440130521
607271BV00006B/501

IT'S BEDTIME!

A Platt & Munk **ALL ABOARD BOOK**™

IT'S

Platt & Munk, Publishers

Text copyright © 1987 by Dina Anastasio.
Illustrations copyright © 1987 by Lucinda
McQueen. All rights reserved. This All Aboard
edition published in 1989 by Platt & Munk,
Publishers, a division of Grosset & Dunlap.
Grosset & Dunlap is a member of The Putnam
Publishing Group, New York. ALL ABOARD
BOOKS is a trademark of The Putnam Publishing
Group. Published simultaneously in Canada.
Printed in the U.S.A. Library of Congress Catalog
Card Number: 88-83630 ISBN 0-448-34331-2
ABCDEFGHIJ

The contents of this book have
previously appeared in *Bedtime Stories,*
published by Grosset & Dunlap.

BEDTIME!

FIVE FAVORITE NURSERY TALES

Retold by Dina Anastasio

Illustrated by Lucinda McQueen

Goldilocks and the Three Bears

Once upon a time there were three bears who lived in a house in the woods. One was a great big Papa Bear, one was a middle-sized Mama Bear, and the last was a wee small Baby Bear.

One day, the bear family made porridge for breakfast. While the porridge cooled, the bears went for a walk in the woods. After they were gone, a little girl named Goldilocks came upon the bears' house. Being curious, she opened the door and went in.

Goldilocks was hungry, so she was happy to see three bowls full of porridge on the table.

First she tasted the porridge in the great big bowl, but it was too hot. Then she tried the porridge in the middle-sized bowl, but it was too cold. Then she tasted the porridge in the wee small bowl, and it was just right. Goldilocks liked the porridge so much that she ate every bit of it.

Goldilocks went to another room and saw three chairs. She tried to sit in the great big chair, but it was much too hard for her. Then she sat down in the middle-sized chair, but it was too soft. Finally she tried the wee small chair, and it was just right. But no sooner had she plopped herself down than the small chair broke all to pieces.

Goldilocks went upstairs and found a room with three beds in it. Feeling tired, she lay down on the great big bed, but the mattress was too hard for her. Next she tried the middle-sized bed, but it was much too soft. Finally Goldilocks lay down on the wee small bed, and it was just right. So she covered herself up and fell fast asleep.

By this time the three bears had come home to their breakfast. Papa Bear saw a spoon in his porridge bowl. "SOMEBODY HAS BEEN EATING MY PORRIDGE!" said Papa Bear in his great big voice.

Then Mama Bear saw a spoon in her bowl, too. "SOMEBODY HAS BEEN EATING *MY* PORRIDGE!" said Mama Bear in her middle-sized voice.

When Baby Bear saw his little bowl, he cried out in a wee small voice, "SOMEBODY HAS BEEN EATING MY PORRIDGE, AND HAS EATEN IT ALL UP!"

The three bears began to look around. Papa Bear saw that the hard cushion in his great big chair was not straight. "SOMEBODY HAS BEEN SITTING IN MY CHAIR!" he shouted in his great big voice.

Mama Bear saw that the soft cushion in her middle-sized chair was all rumpled. "SOMEBODY HAS BEEN SITTING IN MY CHAIR!" she exclaimed in her middle-sized voice.

When Baby Bear saw what had happened to his chair, he cried out in a wee small voice, "SOMEBODY HAS BEEN SITTING IN MY CHAIR, AND HAS BROKEN IT ALL TO PIECES!"

Then the three bears went upstairs to take a look. Papa Bear saw that someone had wrinkled the cover on his great big bed. "SOMEBODY HAS BEEN LYING IN MY BED!" Papa Bear boomed out in his great big voice.

Mama Bear saw that the cover on her bed was not straight. "SOMEBODY HAS BEEN LYING IN *MY* BED!" said Mama Bear in her middle-sized voice.

And when Baby Bear looked at his bed, there was Goldilocks, fast asleep. "SOMEBODY HAS BEEN LYING IN *MY* BED," cried Baby Bear in his wee small voice, "AND SHE'S STILL HERE!"

The squeaky voice of the wee small bear awakened Goldilocks. When she saw the three bears looking down at her, she jumped out of bed, raced down the stairs, and ran out of the house as fast as she could.

Since Goldilocks never returned, the three bears never saw the little girl again.

The City Mouse and the Country Mouse

There was once a mouse—a plain, sensible sort of mouse—who lived by himself far out in the country. One day a friend who lived in the city came to visit him. The Country Mouse served his friend a supper of freshly picked peas, golden corn, and a bit of cheddar cheese. The City Mouse only picked at what was served—a nibble here and a nibble there—wondering how his friend could enjoy such plain food.

After dinner the City Mouse said to the Country Mouse, "My good friend, how can you be happy here in the country? There is no fun here, no gaiety. Everything is dull and humdrum—even the food. Why don't you come with me to the city and see the exciting life that I lead?"

The Country Mouse agreed, and as soon as it was dark, they started off for the city. They arrived in time to learn that a splendid dinner was being given in the mansion where the City Mouse lived. When the guests left the dining room, the servants took the leftover food to the big pantry.

The two mice, who had been waiting in the pantry, began feasting as soon as the door was shut. There was juicy roast beef and delicious gravy, plump rolls and bowls of salad. The Country Mouse could hardly believe his eyes!

Suddenly the door opened, and a maid came into the pantry. The two mice hid behind the flour bin while she bustled about. When she was gone, the friends returned to their feast.

Once again the door opened, and a boy looking for a piece of cake rushed in, followed by his noisy dog.

The City Mouse ran to the safety of a mouse hole in the pantry wall, which, by the way, he had not been thoughtful enough to show to his friend. By the time the Country Mouse found the hole, he was trembling with fear and could scarcely calm down. When the City Mouse asked him if he wanted to continue their feast, the Country Mouse shook his tiny head. "Oh, no," he said. "Your exciting city life is too much for me. What I want is peace and quiet in the country."

And with that, the Country Mouse put on his cap, hurried out of the big house, and headed straight for home in the country.

Little Red Riding Hood

In a neat cottage standing by itself at the edge of a forest lived a little girl whose name was Little Red Riding Hood. It wasn't her *real* name, but people called her that because she always wore a bright red velvet cloak and hood that her grandmother had made for her.

One morning after breakfast Red Riding Hood's mother packed a lunch of good things to eat. She filled a basket with apples, oranges, grapes, gingerbread, cookies and jam. "These are for your grandmother, who isn't feeling very well," she told the little girl. "I want you to take this basket to her right away. Just stay on the path as you go through the woods to her house, then give Grandma a kiss for me and one for yourself, and come back as soon as ever you can."

Little Red Riding Hood was happy to visit her grandmother, since she loved her dearly, so she took the basket and set out. As she entered the forest, however, a wolf suddenly appeared on the path.

"Good morning, little girl," said the wolf in his gruff voice. "And where might you be going this fine day?"

Now the wolf was no friend, and Red Riding Hood should not have said a word. Instead she answered, "I'm bringing this basket of goodies to my sick Grandma who lives on the other side of the forest."

Well, that was all the wicked wolf had to know to make plans of his own. He would get to the grandmother's house before Little Red Riding Hood.

"See the pretty flowers growing all around us," said the wolf. "Why not pick some and take them to your grandmother as well?"

Red Riding Hood was sure that her grandmother would be pleased to have a pretty bouquet, so she picked some of the brightest flowers she could see. Meanwhile, the wolf slipped away behind the trees and took a shortcut to the grandmother's house.

And what should the wicked wolf do when he got there but gobble up the old woman, all in one piece! Then he quickly put on her nightclothes and jumped into bed, pretending to be the grandmother.

When Little Red Riding Hood arrived at her grandmother's house and went into the bedroom, she could hardly believe her eyes. "Grandma," she cried. "What big ears you have!"

"The better to hear you with, my dear," the wolf replied.

"Grandma, what big eyes you have!" said Little Red Riding Hood.

"The better to see you with, my dear," answered the wolf.

"And, Grandma, what big teeth you have!"

"The better to eat you with!" the wolf growled, leaping out of bed. And before the little girl could say anything more, she was swallowed in one greedy gulp.

With a doubly full stomach, the wicked wolf crawled back into bed, closed his eyes, and was soon snoring loudly.

It so happened just at this time that a hunter was passing by the house. When he heard the sound of loud snoring, he decided to take a look inside. And when he saw the wolf fast

asleep in Grandmother's bed, he knew exactly what had happened. He took out his hunting knife and in a moment cut open the bulging stomach of the wicked wolf. In the very next moment Little Red Riding Hood sprang out.

The grandmother was quite safe, too, and was happy to see her grandchild. Then they all sat down to a picnic lunch, since there was enough food in the basket for all, and the flowers Red Riding Hood had picked surely did cheer up her grandmother.

Best of all, the forest was free of the wicked wolf, for which everyone felt most particularly thankful!

The Little Red Hen

Once upon a time there was a Little Red Hen who found some grains of wheat.

"Who will help me plant this wheat?" the Little Red Hen asked the other animals in the barnyard.

"Not I," growled the Dog.

"Not I," meowed the Cat.

"Not I," grunted the Pig.

"Then I will plant this wheat all by myself," clucked the Little Red Hen.

She planted the wheat, and before long it grew tall and yellow.

"Who will help me cut and thresh the wheat?" the Little Red Hen asked the animals in the barnyard.

"Not I," growled the Dog.

"Not I," meowed the Cat.

"Not I," grunted the Pig.

"Then I will cut and thresh the wheat all by myself," clucked the Little Red Hen.

The Little Red Hen cut the wheat and threshed it and gathered it all up in a sack.

Then she spoke to her friends again. "Who will help me take the wheat to the mill?" asked the Little Red Hen.

"Not I," growled the Dog.

"Not I," meowed the Cat.

"Not I," grunted the Pig.

"Then I will take the wheat to the mill all by myself," clucked the Little Red Hen.

She carried the sack all the way to the mill and watched the miller grind the wheat into flour. When she finally came back, the Little Red Hen said to the others, "Who will help me mix this flour into dough, so that I can bake some bread?"

"Not I," growled the Dog.

"Not I," meowed the Cat.

"Not I," grunted the Pig.

"Then I will mix the dough and bake the bread all by myself," clucked the Little Red Hen.

When the bread was baked, a delicious smell filled the barnyard. The animals gathered around the Little Red Hen. "Who will help me eat this bread?" she asked them.

"I will!" barked the Dog.

"I will!" purred the Cat.

"I will!" squealed the Pig.

"No, you won't," said the Little Red Hen, tying a napkin around her neck. "I planted the wheat by myself. I cut and threshed it. I took it to the mill. I mixed the dough and baked the bread all by myself. Now I will eat the bread—all by myself."

And that's just what she did!

The Three Little Pigs

There was once a mother pig who had three little pigs. When the little pigs were old enough, their mother sent them off to seek their fortunes.

The first little pig met a man with a bundle of straw. He said to the man, "Please, sir, give me some straw to build a house."

The man gave him some straw, and the little pig built a house with it. Soon a wolf came and knocked on the door.

"Little pig, little pig, let me come in," said the wolf.

But the pig answered, "No, not by the hair of my chinny-chin-chin."

And the wolf said, "Then I'll huff, and I'll puff, and I'll blow your house in." So he huffed . . . and he puffed . . . and he blew the house in. Then he gobbled up the first little pig.

The second little pig met a man with a bundle of sticks, and he said, "Please, sir, give me some sticks to build a house."

The man gave him some sticks, and the pig built a house with them. Then along came the very same wolf and said, "Little pig, little pig, let me come in."

"No, not by the hair of my chinny-chin-chin."

"Then I'll huff, and I'll puff, and I'll blow your house in," said the wolf. He huffed . . . and he puffed . . . and at last he blew the house in. Then he gobbled up the second little pig.

The third little pig met a man with a load of bricks, and he said, "Please, sir, give me some bricks to build a house."

So the man gave him some bricks, and the pig built a strong house for himself. Along came the wolf, saying, "Little pig, little pig, let me come in."

"No, not by the hair of my chinny-chin-chin," said the third little pig.

"Then I'll huff, and I'll puff, and I'll blow your house in," said the wolf.

Well, he huffed . . . and he puffed . . . and he puffed . . . and he huffed, but he could *not* blow the house in. He said slyly, "Little pig, I know where there is a nice field of turnips."

"Where?" asked the little pig.

"I'll be glad to show you tomorrow," said the wolf. "Be ready at six o'clock in the morning, and I will call for you. Then we will go pick turnips together."

"Very well," said the little pig.

But the little pig knew where the turnip field was, so he rose at five and went to get turnips by himself. When the wolf arrived at the little pig's house at six, the little pig was back safe at home.

The wolf was very angry when he learned that the little pig already had a potful of turnips for his dinner. Then he thought of a new trick.

"Little pig," said the wolf, "I know where there is a nice apple tree."

"Where?" said the pig.

"I will come for you at five o'clock tomorrow morning," said the wolf, "and show you where the apple tree is."

But the little pig knew exactly where the apple tree could be found, so he awakened at four o'clock the next morning and went off for apples. The wolf got up early, too, however, and arrived at the apple tree to find the pig up in the tree, still picking apples. Seeing the wolf, the little pig became very frightened.

The wolf called up to him, "Little pig! You *are* an early riser! Are the apples good?"

"Yes, very," said the little pig. "I will throw one down to you. You may judge for yourself."

But the pig threw the apple so far that the wolf had to run and get it. The little pig had only enough time to jump down from the tree and race home.

The next day the wolf came to the pig's house again. "Little pig," he said, "the county fair begins this afternoon. Will you go?"

"Oh, yes," said the pig. "What time shall I be ready?"

"At three," said the wolf.

So the little pig left his house long before three and got to the fair and bought a butter churn. He was on his way home when he saw the wolf coming up a hill toward him. The little pig jumped into the churn to hide, but the churn fell over and rolled down the hill. The strange object rolled toward the wolf, frightening him so much that he ran home without going to the fair.

Later he went to the little pig's house and told him about the big round thing that had come rolling down the hill. The little pig laughed and told the wolf about the butter churn he had bought at the fair.

The wolf had been tricked again! Now he was so angry that he climbed up to the roof of the little pig's house. From there he would slide down the chimney and gobble the pig at last.

When the little pig heard the wolf on the roof, he hung a pot of water in the fireplace and quickly lit a blazing fire. Just as the wolf came down the chimney, the little pig took the cover off the boiling pot. PLOP! The wolf dropped in.

That was the end of the wolf. This is the end of the story!